BILL SALUGA'S NAME GAME BOOK by Bill Saluga
HOW TO SPEAK SOUTHERN by Steve Mitchell
HOW TO TALK COUNTRY by Doug Todd
THE LARRY WILDE BOOK OF LIMERICKS by Larry Wilde
THE *Last* OFFICIAL JEWISH JOKE BOOK by Larry Wilde
THE LOTUS POSITION by Lotus Weinstock
More THE OFFICIAL SEX MANIACS JOKE BOOK by Larry Wilde
THE OFFICIAL DOCTORS JOKE BOOK by Larry Wilde
THE OFFICIAL LAWYERS JOKE BOOK by Larry Wilde
THE UNKNOWN COMIC'S SCRAPBAG by Murray Langston
WOULD YOU BELIEVE? by Don Adams and Bill Dana

THE LOTUS POSITION

Thoughts that survived the 60's, 70's, and 80's.

By Lotus Weinstock

A Dana/Corwin Publication

Produced by Bill Dana and Stan Corwin

Illustrated by Norman Klein

Editorial Direction by Meg Staahl and Shelley Weinstock

BANTAM BOOKS
TORONTO · NEW YORK · LONDON · SYDNEY

THE LOTUS POSITION

A Bantam Book / August 1982

All rights reserved.
Copyright © 1982 by Dana/Corwin Enterprises, Inc.
Cover photo by Nurit Wilde

Book designed by Gene Siegel.

ISBN 0-553-14807-9

Published simultaneously in the United States and Canada

Bantam Books are published by Bantam Books, Inc. Its trademark,
consisting of the words "Bantam Books" and the portrayal of a
rooster, is Registered in U.S. Patent and Trademark Office and in
other countries. Marca Registrada. Bantam Books, Inc., 666 Fifth
Avenue, New York, New York 10103.

PRINTED IN THE UNITED STATES OF AMERICA

0 9 8 7 6 5 4 3 2 1

CONTENTS

2201807

INTRODUCTION

It is important to know that Lotus's mother dropped her on her head three times. Once in a supermarket and twice in Times Square on New Year's Eve. There the child was trampled and kicked into a cheap souvenir shop where she was on sale for twelve years.

It was there that she learned to tap-dance on shark teeth with carrots stuck in her ears.

An unemployed dirigible commander fell madly in love with her, ate her carrots, and hid her tap shoes.

They ran away to Ep, an obscure island in the South Pacific where the only industry is embalming dead beetles which are then stuck on paper clips to make them decorative.

Lotus soon tired of Beetle-a-balmia *and* the commander. So she snuck out one night, swimming all the way to Los Angeles under cover of darkness. It's a good thing it was dark. You should see her body! Once ashore she became a hit overnight as a comic. Her body helped.

And once this book hits the stands, she will be a best-selling author. I say "Hip Hip Hooray, Lotus!"

Phyllis Diller

Dedication

This is dedicated to those . . .
Who carried flowers and peace signs in the '60's,
    herpes and grudges in the '70's, and high hopes
    and tear gas in the '80's . . .
Whose first gay affair was their only,
Who had an abortion in Puerto Rico,
Who force themselves to go to museums on Sundays
    and leave ten minutes later saying, "I'll be back
    . . ." but never return.
Who thought Woodstock was a great idea but
    couldn't hack the crowds . . .
Who missed meat the entire time they were vegetarian,
To those who when recording their checks, round them
    off to the nearest dollar . . .
Who didn't flip for the Beatles till "Rubber Soul,"
Who felt guilty for making love the night JFK was
    shot—
Who paid dearly for free love,
Who didn't force flowers on everybody during the
    '60's because they knew some people had hay
    fever,
Who didn't try to understand Dylan's one hundred
    tenth dream, but wished him well . . .
Who had no trouble understanding Lenny Bruce,
Who felt too guilty to make love the night Lennon
    was shot,
Who loved Tim Hardin's music so much they had to
    write their own,
Who have the right to dream about Woody Allen,

Who understand the difference between humor and
    ridicule,
Who care about keeping up with the times but have
    no desire to learn metrics,
Who deny ever having taken drugs since Reagan was
    elected,
Who were jealous of the Boat People for having
    great skin, fabulous bone structure, not an ounce
    of fat, and an oceanfront view,
Who care as much about adding life to their years as
    years to their life.

But

This is not for people who can fill out their own
    tax return.

Dear Reader:

It's later than it's ever been and I've been wanting to talk to you for a long time. My name is Lotus Weinstock and I have so much to tell you! Let me start by giving you a few brief facts about myself so you can really relate to my point of view.

First of all, I'm an average, semiliberated woman. You know the term liberated; semiliberated means I don't wear underwear but I'm frigid, and my favorite love song in the '70's was "Help Me Fake It Through The Night" . . . Just a joke . . . I do wear underwear, but only when I make love. Humor! It should be declared the sixth sense! Without it, I might have been just another disillusioned flower child or a casualty of mind expansion with stretch marks on my brain.

You might be wondering how someone with a last name like Weinstock has a first name like Lotus. My mother took acid, in the '40's. She was looking for a headache cure . . . The truth is, my real name is Marlena Weinstock, but in 1970 I joined a spiritual organization which was the cheapest form of therapy available at the time. They were a fabulous bunch! So Aquarian . . . I loved their look! Long white monks' cloth dresses that didn't show your thighs, and it's a good thing because they ate lots of guacamole, dates, and cheesecake.

Everyone gave deep foot massages without giving you the feeling that as soon as they were finished you'd have to give one right back. They said I was perfect. I thought they were high . . . They were!

I asked, "How do I become a member?" They said: "Give us your car and change your name."

No, I did not give them a Lotus. (God forbid I

should have been named after the car I gave them, Pontiac Weinstock?) They said, "Take the name Lotus; you'll get new vibes." The lotus is an ancient mystical symbol of enlightenment, a flower whose fragrance induces forgetfulness, an aphrodisiac, all the qualities I so desired. "Take it, take it, you'll grow into it!" Turns out lotus means low tush, and I am growing into it. It's a good thing your head gets higher as your body gets lower. Oh, gravity, gravity! I'm so annoyed with gravity. Now there's another law I wouldn't mind amending.

Actually my name is more than merely a souvenir of the 60's. Lotus represents my spiritual aspirations and Weinstock my earthly: Lotus, the California cosmic; Weinstock, the Philadelphia Jewish. Lotus, the yin; Weinstock, the yang. Lotus is right brained; Weinstock is left. Lotus is spirit; Weinstock is flesh. Lotus explores outer space; Weinstock is into inner space. Lotus is the witness; Weinstock, the participant. The paradox of persona!

Lotus likes to channel wisdom; Weinstock wants to tell jokes and hates rejection. Lotus knows there's no such thing as rejection, only varying degrees of affinity; Weinstock says, "Bullshit." Lotus knows she's not her body; Weinstock can't wait for everyone else to find out. Lotus wants to be totally free; Weinstock will settle for a discount. Weinstock loves to eat white fish and bagels a lot; Lotus will only eat that when the moon is in Pisces and the bagels are whole wheat (which is good for Weinstock because that stuff can kill you). Lotus is the believer; Weinstock, the skeptic.

So, Lotus works for Weinstock, and since Lotus loves to laugh, in that sense, Weinstock works for Lotus, too, but when Weinstock and Lotus are working together, I experience a sort of "be-here-nowishness." Of course, Weinstock calls it atonement; Lotus calls it at-one-ment; and Bill Dana calls it the ability to write a short book.

Imagine . . . me, writing a book! . . . me . . . who doesn't even know what it is I do until I'm doing it . . . me, who had a nose job before Streisand made it!

It seems that for approximately seven minutes out of every day I know everything I need to know . . . and I'm able to connect all the pieces of the puzzle in a most amazing fashion. You'd think by now, in my thirty-seventh time around the sun I'd know enough to have a pencil with me at all times, so I could record my genius as proof to my husband that I am not a total write-off who spends all my time just looking for my keys and taking baths.

I never know when the clarity will strike . . . quite often it happens when I'm driving and I desperately slop through the glove compartment for something to write with, but I never get past the leaking flashlight batteries and gas receipts which I saved because someone told me to for tax purposes or something . . . and mostly because it makes me feel like I'm finally taking responsibility for my life . . . GOD I'm really a basket case . . . ever since I flunked reading that first semester in first grade . . . I knew I'd never get to be a grown-up . . .

With all the transcendental experiences I've had (as Lotus) I, (Weinstock) always wake up holding that disastrous report card.

However, since my viewpoint is constantly changing I should mention that I also consider myself to be a person of infinite depth with the most important values . . .

Example:
I used to study with the Jehovah's Witnesses in

1973. One afternoon, my favorite Witness had convinced me that Armageddon was so imminent that I thought surely it would be announced on the seven o'clock news . . . film at eleven.

I remember stocking up on necessities.

I bought two large bags of brown rice, eighteen bottles of head shampoo, and twelve packets of Max Factor cake rouge (Misty Rose). (I thought: "I'm going through this holocaust with clean hair and pink cheeks.") I've never missed a day of wearing rouge since summer camp of '57. Even when I was totally organic, I used the juice from a beet to pinken my narrow face.

In case you're wondering why I thought any of this was worth mentioning—

trust me, I have a purpose!

Besides, it's not a large commitment. It's not like I'm asking you to read Tolstoy's version of War and Peace, *just mine.*

* * *

Please view these pages as bread crumbs on the path of my experience. I'm counting on them to get me out of the woods.

Fondly,

Lotus Weinstock

POSITIONS

ON LIFE:
The Main Event

Life is a picture with infinite exposure . . .

ON PAIN:
The Rack

If pain is a rich man's pleasure, I've been living beyond my means!

The question oft arises, can we feel another's pain? I'll never forget the time my husband accidentally* closed a vaultlike door on my hand. The more it swelled the more he cried, "It's my hand . . . it's my hand . . ." I remember thinking how at-one we'd become. At last we'd transcended not only spiritual, but physical separateness.

Upon returning home from the emergency ward, my husband composed a most touching love song on the piano, in tribute to our newfound unity . . . The song was titled "It's My Hand."

*See ON ACCIDENTS: The Unconscious Design.

The warmth of our closeness crescendoed as his fingers played that last arpeggio and suddenly I realized . . . *It was not his hand* . . . just as I had realized ten years prior, during the birth of our daughter, that he was in fact *not pregnant* . . . the moral o' the story . . .

> *it's my pain but he can cry if he wants to* . . .

* * *

Women are built to bear incredible pain . . . if there's none to be had, we know how to create it! We must feel like we are giving birth to something . . . Whether it's a problem, an idea, or a baby.

* * *

There's such certainty in emotional pain for everyone. Like a loyal friend—or a credit card that you can't leave home without—it's accepted all over the world—so if you lose it, don't worry, there's a branch in every corner of the planet (at harm's length). Keep in mind, however, American pain has a painfully low rate of exchange on the Asian pain market.

* * *

If there wasn't any pain in the world, we'd all be getting unemployment, for instance, doctors, lawyers, pharmacists, psychiatrists, filmmakers, comics, insurance salesmen, coal miners, electricians, and all who profit in our hour of need (morticians!) . . .

The economy depends on pain.

In fact there is the new designer-pain from Darvon-i . . . very '80's—very psycho-illogical; created by Self . . . clings to your every desire, fashioned to fit the American Dream . . .

* * *

Here's a little quiz to see how painfully creative you are:

Let's start with a perfect situation! . . .

You have just won a free trip to Hawaii, with all expenses paid.

Now:

Is it a chance to get away from it all, so when you return, your teenager will . . .
a. appreciate you more
b. need an abortion

Is it that long-awaited opportunity for your house to be . . .
a. painted
b. robbed

A chance to fall in love and find new reason to . . .
a. live
b. die (because your wife/ husband will kill you)

A chance to get that fabulous coveted Hawaiian tan and return to the ooh's and ah's of . . .
a. PTA
b. AMA (skin cancer division)

If you answered *b* to all of these questions—you've won your "designer-pain" insurance policy which protects you against two of your primal fears—the Fear of Falling and the Fear of Loneliness. Since you have already hit rock bottom there is no where else to fall and it's only lonely at the top.

P.S. Always remember your pain is proof that you are not dead— A critical sign of life.

* * *

If cold is the absence of heat, pain is the absence of pleasure . . .

* * *

People who master their emotions are able to find the pain in the pleasure and the pleasure in the pain— I think they call that the "middle path."

Very Lotus

* * *

Weinstock wants to take people's pain away from them— Lotus says that would be depriving them of their growth! After all, "Smooth seas never made the skilled mariner."

* * *

To me the best cure for emotional or psychological hurt is a good toothache! When I was little Marlena Weinstock and I complained of mental anguish, my grandmother would tell me to hit my head against the wall so when I stopped it would feel good! . . . My grandmother died of a brain concussion but she had a smile on her face . . . and a twinkle in her third eye.

* * *

ON SYMPATHY:
The Damaging Reward

"Show me a person who loves to suffer and I'll show you a person who's hooked on sympathy."

Recently I heard someone say, "You don't get points for suffering." I disagree! My mother was never nicer than when I was burning with fever. She'd kiss my forehead gently and say, "How about a baked potato, mumala?" I was sick a lot! I don't reward my daughter's suffering with too much sympathy. Don't get me wrong, I don't slap her around and say things like, "You disgusting sick person."

I merely slip her food under the door with some flat sterno and say, "Cook it yourself and see me when you're better—"

She's rarely sick!

ON ACCIDENTS:
The Unconscious Design

"There are no accidents in the universe."
I read that and that was no accident!
It was in a book I stumbled upon accidentally.

ON BUSING:
The Cosmic Caboose

I'd like to see busing based on astrological signs. Too many Geminis at one school? Bus them! Let them mingle with a Taurus or a Sagg! Get to know the other half of the zodiac!

ON ASTROLOGY:
The Astral Clock

Astrology is a clock . . . but G.O.D.* is the tick . . . and God said: "Thou shalt have no other gods before me." He said nothing about after—just don't worship the stars— acknowledge them.

---

*GOD: G = Generator, O = Organizer, D = Destroyer

ON PARANOIA:
The Ugly Truth

I never met a paranoid person who wasn't being talked about!

Dearest Reader,

Keep in mind while reading "My Position" on marriage—that I celebrate the sweetest moments in song, . . .

While the saltier ones seek refuge in my jokes! (between the punch lines) I made a deal with my husband— I'd put up with his Vesuvian behavior as long as he didn't mind if I told the rest of the world about it. If you knew him you'd say he got a good deal—

ON MARRIAGE:
The ~~Promise~~ Com-promise

In order to be the kind of woman who's strong enough to live with a man, it makes you the kind of woman no man wants to live with!

Let me run that by you again . . . In order to be the kind of person who is strong enough to live with another person, it makes you the kind of person that no other person wants to live with!

I believe in marriage; it's very '90's.

To me it's so comforting to know that when I'm really depressed, in a heavy self-doubt mode, I can always depend on the same man to be there beside me, to honestly make me feel even a little worse about myself. He's amazing that way. I mean, there have been times when I couldn't possibly have felt any worse and he found a way. Yet I wouldn't want a relationship where a man constantly told me I was beautiful and totally together.

You don't grow when there's no conflict.

* * *

I'm determined to make my marriage work. I read everything I can on how to sustain the love past the "early stages" where you wash your hair more often and you have to change your outfit twice a day.

I just read in a woman's report that 83 per cent of the fights that occur between married people happen during the week of the monthly blues . . . ring any bells, gals?*

My husband says that for that week I'm impossible to get along with!

Makes me mad, but if I'm honest, I have to admit that for that week I do exactly like he does for the rest of the month. When my husband and I were first married he wouldn't let me cook dinner during "that week." I was so totally insulted till I realized that I had a great thing going. I told him I had it all the time. Now the man is a great cook.

* * *

I think one of the reasons the attraction wears off between married people is that we forget to kiss. We forget how much of the romance begins with the lips.

I know for me there's a Watts line from my mouth to my na-na, but my husband thinks foreplay is a form of begging. Well, he used to until a sex therapist

*G.A.L.: G = genuine, A = altruistic, L = logical

turned my honey and me on to a brand-new position that's got us real excited again. It's very '80's. Very Reaganesque . . . very postmedfly . . . post budget cuts . . . Are you ready? It's where the man gets *on top* of the woman.

* * *

Relationships are so difficult to sustain. Sometimes I wonder how our parents did it without heavy drugs. (Or maybe they didn't). But I can truthfully say I think my husband and I have found the secret to a successful marriage. We don't live together. We never have. (Except on weekends, Valentine's Day and Martin Luther King, Jr.'s, Birthday) He lives five blocks away from me. It was not my idea at first. It's very hard on a woman to always be the biggest person in the house, especially during pregnancy and that intense nesting drive. But . . . he wasn't ready for children. It was the late '60's and he didn't think it was cosmic enough, since his parents had done it.

Now, I wouldn't trade this arrangement for longer legs! We found the distance where our moods don't sting.

A lot of people immediately assume that we have an "open marriage." My husband's very liberated that way. He says I can have an open relationship with any man as long as the relationship's not *mental* . . . or *physical,* of course . . . or *spiritual* or *emotional.* If the person's in a coma, I can be as open as I want.

How could I live with a man that counts the amount of toilet paper I use? He claims he can tell from the other room by the sound of the revolutions the roll makes. He hears "Ch-ch-ch." He screams "That's enough, honey." He doesn't realize that women have twice as much to deal with. I hope that doesn't come

13

as a shock. If so, please read *The Hite Report.* Three thousand women revealed the most intimate things about themselves, including that. What a blessing! We were in the dark for so long about our processes. In fact, there was a whole chapter devoted to women who don't know if they ever had an orgasm. One woman actually said she heard that when you had one you were supposed to see flashing lights and your back was supposed to arch.

Forgive me for laughing but I figure you could be driving along Sunset Boulevard at night and rear-end someone and think you just had an orgasm!

No wonder some women fall in love with their cars. They call it orgasm. I call it whiplash!

* * *

In my clearest moments, when I'm counting my blessings, I realize I married Mr. Right. Mr. *Always* Right! He can't even get a wrong number. The man thinks if I'm right, that makes him wrong. He does not yet realize that in this vast universe there can be two totally different viewpoints which are both right.

* * *

My husband and I met at a "love-in" and saw the perfection in each other. We said, "Let's get married and save the world." We got married . . . and saved the world . . . from each other.

I don't mean to give the impression that my husband is impossible to get along with, because at times he's one of the most giving men on this planet and I remember those two times so vividly. Last Valentine's Day he sent me the most beautiful anonymous valentine. I knew it was from him 'cause there was no stamp on it. He's spiritually extravagant, like he gives free advice freely, and last year he gave

14

me an ulcer! He's a songwriter of psalmlike sweet-
ness, a genius, and *very* handsome, which justifies his
compulsive behavior (to him). He's dangerously
safe—or is it safely dangerous? . . . If he should throw
a vase, it would land on a pillow, though I might be
napping on it at the time. He's perfect for my addiction
to crises. I was raised on them. My mother is a Pisces
. . . Pisces and crises, they rhyme for a reason . . .
remember there are no accidents in the universe. He's
the best and he's the worst. The most extreme.
Thank God he doesn't pinch tushies, but pennies are
another story. The man is the type, if he has eight
minutes left on the parking meter, he'll wait it out. No
one else will get his three cents' worth. In case of
nuclear attack, he'd take the meter with him. He thinks
it's extravagant to change your socks every day. He'll
actually wear the same socks four days straight . . . in
running shoes . . . Toxic Socks Syndrome! I once
put Odor Eaters in his socks; they're now on Weight
Watchers . . . If I could bottle that scent it would be
safe for women to hitchhike again!

* * *

But it's so easy to pick on your mate, and yet your
mate is the one who sees you through the hardships.
The one who has to look at your morning face. The
one whose feet we should kiss. I kissed my husband's
feet once, and was I sorry.

* * *

If you want your relationship to last, I suggest you
pluck the word "fair" out of your vocabulary (by the
roots). That is, if "fair" implies that you expect
the other person to contribute what you contribute. It's
the seed of disagreement. The subtext of every
argument I've had with my husband is— "You don't

know how hard it is to be me," —and so I'm forced
to make his life a little harder, just so he understands.
There's purpose in my motive. It's not just revenge,
though that happens to be a side benefit . . .

* * *

Watching TV with my husband is pure torture . . ."
Not only does he sit directly in front of the screen in
order to adjust the color for oh maybe twelve to fifteen
minutes at a time (his greatest show of patience), but
once the flesh tone is where he wants it, he begins to
flick from channel to channel for the kaleidoscope
effect which is a holdover from the '60's (he used to
run the light shows). He claims his technique acts as
an oracle. "A sentence from this show, and a sentence
from that show, will tell us what's really going on in
the higher realms."

The only thing that stops him is a *Rockford Files*
rerun or my saying, "We have nothing together . . .
Let's end the misery" . . . at which time he puts on
his blue-black sweater (that's become the symbol of
our differences), with such velocity that it propels him
to the door and I am once again left sitting alone in a
pool of resentment, while my stomach fills with the
acid of disbelief at the thought that I helped to create
this in my reality.

My ESTian friends tell me I must love the drama or I
wouldn't attract it . . . *No!!!! No!!!! No!!!!* I just like to
watch one show at a time . . . Call me a linear thinker
or militant feminist but I think I have the right to
voice *my* opinion in *my* bedroom, where I pay *my*
money to *my* landlord because *MY* husband wanted
it that way in the first place . . .

Ah . . . but once again Providence provides me
with the opportunity to transcend the pettiness of both

our "little me's" and in doing so burn up some past karma . . . so I call him because by now he should be home. It only takes two minutes fifty-three seconds for him to get there when he's mad at me.

HIM: "Hello."

ME: "Hello."

I search for the remorse in his voice knowing once he gets that sweater off he'll see he's been selfish to his soul mate. I say, "Honey, you're such a great man and to whom more is given, more is expected . . . So if you could just ask me if I'd mind before you change channels, it would help me to feel like I am actually in the room with you. Then I wouldn't be forced to make such a fuss in order to get your attention."

By now he's got his own TV on and I'm watching Carson with the sound off (though I managed to lose the color) so we don't feel as victimized by each other! We're able to squeak out an "I love you" silently blessing the fact that we are a two-TV family (even though his is much newer) . . . If only there weren't five blocks between our Zeniths, now would be the perfect time to kiss . . . But it will have to wait for the weekend . . .

FEBRUARY 14, 1982: HEARTS AND DARTS

My husband doesn't love Weinstock today. Conceptually, he always loves Lotus. Lotus is on the pedestal. Weinstock's underneath it. Lotus doesn't evoke the dominant Jewish mother experience in him. She gets

the eternally romantic songs written about her . . .
Lotus gets the valentines . . . the hearts, but Weinstock
gets the darts— To Weinstock he's chronically antago-
nistic. A nostril dilating emotional button pusher, and
he's forever pushing my two main buttons— The
only thing I haven't figured out yet is how you can be
both frigid and a slut— Of course Weinstock is
nobody's dart board— She pushes his main button
right back— I say, "You sleep more than I do." It
drives him crazy— But fighting with your mate can be
beneficial. My husband furnished my house with
guilt. After each argument he'd bring home a chair or a
table. Sort of gravestones for dead issues. Now we
have an agreement, never go to bed angry at each
other. I haven't slept in weeks.

* * *

But when you think that you know everything about
a person that there is to know, that's when the true
mystery begins; because what you don't know about
them is what hasn't happened to them yet.

* * *

Questions I'm often asked about my marriage
arrangement other than, is it an "open marriage?"

1. **Q:** Is it true that you live five blocks away from
   each other or is it a joke?
   A: Yes to both of those—
   It is true and it is a joke.
2. **Q:** Don't you miss sleeping with him?
   A: What you don't know you don't miss!
   Besides, when he sleeps here—we don't sleep—
   Reason—I live on a main street. I've trained
   myself to hear the roar of the traffic as though
   it were waves slapping against the shore. My

18

husband, however, can't sleep if there is a fly in the neighborhood.

This keeps him *ultra*-tense—which keeps me *ultra*-up—I can't stand the sound of him being annoyed at the sounds in my neighborhood.

3. **Q:** Do you cook for him every night?
   A: I used to, but since he knows I cook organically he looks upon my meals as though they are medicinal. Something he should eat with a spoonful of sugar.

4. **Q:** Do you have keys to each other's place?
   A: He has one to mine. I don't have one to his—

5. **Q:** Isn't that unfair?
   A: I've plucked that word out of my vocabulary . . . remember?

6. **Q:** Do you do his laundry?
   A: No!
   There was a time when I thought he didn't love or trust me because he wouldn't let me launder his clothes. I begged him to give me a sock, at least to darn. For my thirty-third birthday he yielded. The sock was so hard I broke the needle. But I have no right to complain, I probably have the best thing going— The man feeds himself—does his laundry himself—makes his bed himself, and quite honestly, sometimes I wish he'd go fuck* himself.

7. **Q:** Why do you stay with him if he's so difficult?
   A: "Because he's my man. I love him so. He'll never know. . . ." because I'll never tell him; he'd use it against me.

---

*Sorry, Mom. Just tear this page out before you give it to the rabbi.

ADVANTAGES OF THIS ARRANGEMENT

1. It's one of the few marriages that wouldn't suffer any reality breaks in the event of divorce—except for the fact that I'm pretty sure I'd die if he ever left—

* * *

THE GOOD DREAM

My husband and I were batting a thousand as cocreators of The Perfect Marriage. Both of us working to maintain our individual purposes. We were productive and winning with our products. Both striving for enlightenment and liberation as well as a continuity with the past. We knew that all time must belong to us before we could belong to the times.

Sex between us was rare as a hen's tooth but when it happened, it was *Emmanuel* . . . in the most orthodox sense . . . garters and boas . . . teacher and pupil . . . mother and child . . . hooker and shy boy . . . candy and doctor . . . all things erotic . . . The only thing that interfered with our lovemaking was a mad dash to the typewriter to write a fabulous insight down . . . with a view to a film . . .

* * *

ON RAPE:
The Rude Awakening

Use a Woman—Go to Hell!

I live in the heart of Hollywood, in a first-floor apartment, in a building that was built the same year as the Edsel with the same success. Having lived in a secluded garden house for six years prior to its demolition, with "brothers and sisters" of a like-minded path on either side of me, I was innocent, or rather ignorant of the responsibility connected with an easily accessible apartment dwelling. In fact, I left the garden house door unlocked the entire six years I was there and the worst thing that ever happened to me was that someone secretly left an ugly throw rug on my floor . . . as a gift!

I was protected and I knew it!

When I decided to rent the cottage cheese ceilinged

apartment, I was desperate to find a place. The day I moved from the garden house the bulldozer nearly ran over my shoes. My main consideration was to recreate an outdoor ambience in this shrubless encampment. After first and last, a cleaning fee, and a pet fee (we had a goldfish), I had a few hundred dollars to play with. Other than a complete set of paper dishware, my main investment was in twenty plants and two sets of yellow, flowered gingham curtains that create the illusion of spring— I so need to feel organic. It never occurred to me that you could see through the curtains at night, if you really tried. My bedroom faces an elderly couple's garage and I couldn't imagine they would risk climbing the fenced gas meters under my window just to sneak a peek at younger flesh.

In a way, the apartment was luxury living to my daughter and me: two bathrooms (one actually works), and a kitchen with a sink! The garden house had a sinkless cooking area. I washed the pots in the bathtub, which didn't bother me as much as taking a bath with several grains of buckwheat groats that somehow eluded my sponge. What the new apartment lacked in charm, it made up for in location: four blocks from The Comedy Store, five blocks from my daughter's violin teacher, half a block from Vita Health and Chalet Gourmet, and forty-five feet from every passing stranger. What an opportunity to be more in touch with "the real world." It was good for my craft and satisfying to my soul. A taste of New Yorkness!

It was September 23, 1979, 3:00 A.M. I'd been living here about a year, so life in the busy lane had created its own routine.

As usual, I'd caught the comic on Carson and skimmed through *People* magazine while half listening to Snyder. I faded out during the news reruns so the test pattern was hissing. (I love to sleep under pressure). My husband, who lives five blocks away*, usually calls around 2:10 A.M. to tell me to turn off the TV so I don't burn out the tubes and die from radiation. He didn't call but I wouldn't have heard the phone anyway. It was 103 degrees in the bedroom— one of those California Indian summer nights, where I must be near death before I'm blessed with the mercy of sleep.

Because of the intense heat, I opened my sliding window to about five inches (I couldn't fit my head through and I have the thinnest face in Hollywood). I put the dowel my husband gave me for such occasions at the bottom, and adjusted the lock at the top. I laid down on the bed—kicked away the covers—struggled with my Oz T-shirt—and just managed to remove it when I drifted into the quasars.

I must have been out there for forty-five minutes when a prowler wandered down the one-foot wide weeded alley, leading to the gas meters under my bedroom window. Peering through my gingham curtains, the ones you can see through if you really want to, he viewed my nude physical form in the light of the hissing television. He then proceeded to lift the sliding window out of its slot and wedge it forward, just enough to fit his young wiry body through. *What! A strange man in my bedroom . . . While I'm sleeping naked on my bed?*

OK, I know it sounds like I was asking for it. After all, I was in my bedroom with no clothes.

I should have been sleeping in the shower—lights out!!

*See On Marriage: The ~~Promise~~ Com-promise.

Suddenly I feel a tap on my shoulder, and I look up to see a man I had never before in this life seen.

Well, since it's this life I'm currently worried about losing, I said: *"Agghh!"* To which he replied, "Don't scream, or I'll kill you." I thought, "How unoriginal." Besides, "Agghh" really meant: This is the rudest awakening I have ever experienced. Because I have Libra rising, and I'm compelled to weigh everything, I had to ask myself: "Why was it so rude?"

Well, this man had removed all my choices! — I had *no* choice but to get to know him *immediately*.

And, yet like all of life's paradoxes, within the realm of that choicelessness I still had the choice as to how I was going to handle it!

At first I thought I should sing, "Whenever I feel afraid I hold my head erect."

Then I thought . . . "that's a poor choice! I don't think I want to say 'erect' in front of this man!" I considered asking the casual— "So, where ya from?" but I figured if he really knew where "home" was he probably wouldn't be in my house!

Finally it came to me— "Go for something you have in common— Now— What in Heaven could that be? — You silly . . . GOD . . . talk about the Creator that created both of you!"

More choices!

Should I talk five Books of Moses: *Koran? Kabala?* Bhagavad Gita?*** Buddha? Allah? Jehovah? No!!

"I think I'll talk Jesus—plain, sweet Jesus!"

It's real hard to stay horny when you're talking Jesus—

**Kabala,* the ancient Judaic mystical path to transcendent consciousness
***Bhagavad Gita,* ancient Hindu holy scriptures

Unless, of course, your ethnicity enables you to make it under a dayglow print of the Last Supper.

I kept repeating:

"Jesus loves you!
He wants you to go!
If you go it will be a blessing!
If you stay, it will be hell for eternity!"

It wasn't like I was trying to usurp his power, I just wanted him to use it wisely.

I actually got him to admit that he believed in GOD—just before he put the pillow over my head. At which time, I said, in muffled tones, "I'm beginning to lose trust in you," which may sound like an understatement considering this relationship had no chance from the beginning, though it was clear to me he hadn't accepted the fact.

He kept repeating— "What's your name, baby?"

More choices!

I didn't want to say "Lotus" — I thought he might think it's too "sixties" and want to kill me.

I considered saying "Mary" — but I thought virgins might be his specialty. Nothing too extreme.

So I said, "Marlene" — I dropped the *a* from the end—because it opens up the sound and gives it a more invitational ring.

Then . . . he told me he was leaving—as he straddled me! I thought, "hmmmmmmm . . . this is not the way to the door!"

I couldn't believe it had progressed to this stage.

I usually pattern my crises to stop on this side of "real" danger. I mean, we're talking major scar tissue on my daughter's memory if she wakes up.

I knew then why I'd never asked for my favor from

the universe! I was saving it up for this moment. I mean— I've been in a karmic holding pattern for twelve years—practicing harmlessness ever since my "paradigm shift"—change in consciousness—

Suddenly I felt a new vibration—like a zipper being opened—I wasn't certain if it belonged to the universal portfolio or my intruder's fly! In any case, I knew the conditions were changing. Out of nowhere I heard another voice screaming:

"Move one inch you son of a bitch and I'll blow your fuckin' brains all over the wall."

At first I thought it was my husband who had come to kill me 'cause he found me in bed with a black man.

"What if it's the police and they do shoot his brains out—his brains are so close to mine . . ."

It was the sheriff!

Big macho sheriffs— I loved their "bigness" and their "ballsiness!" I was so glad they were "macho-macho-men"—

My intruder was now curled up at the bottom of my bed like a worm in its precocoon mode.

I flew into my daughter's room who was just waking up from the shouting— I grabbed her . . . kissed her . . . threw her in the closet and said, "Everything's fine:" (Which is what I always do when everything's fine!)

The sound of breaking windows, and orders to open the front door confused me, momentarily—

I was still naked . . . hmmmm

Priorities . . . "should I think about cellulite at a time like this? — No . . . I think not . . ."

So I fluffed my hair out wider than my thighs and I opened the door— "Thank you, Officers . . . I love you . . . I'm sorry about the '60's . . . I never

called you 'pigs' . . . I don't think you killed Lenny
Bruce . . ."

"Thank you— Thank you, Jesus, you do *save*
people . . .

Thank you stand-up comedy . . . you taught me
how to ride my adrenalin in the face of death . . .

Thank you, thank you, my upstairs neighbors for
loving me as you'd love yourself. You're wonderful!
And thank you for listening to your intuition and for
calling the sheriffs—because you heard scratching at
the window and a faint cry of distress . . . and
thank you for being black—so my daughter wouldn't
think a black man equaled "hurt Mommy."

Another experience shared in California!

I was so exhilarated, and so humbled by it all, that I
was filled with compassion for my intruder. I was
certain he'd be born again— I really cared! I prayed,
and he was born again . . . (but) to his wicked
ways—

He told the arresting officer that we'd met at the
supermarket and I invited him over—

Since that time I'm taking no chances—

I just completed a Jewish martial arts course called
Pinchatti—that's where you pinch the attacker to
death, on the jugulars—while you scream, *"You're
such a cutie!!"*

My intruder just completed a year in jail for attempted
burglary— I'll continue praying for him—from my
new(er) apartment.

* * *

P.S. If after reading my first-person story "ON
RAPE: The Rude Awakening," it appears that I am
making *light* of a serious issue, consider instead that

27

I've merely put the issue in a *light* where I don't mind looking at it.

It's enough that the rude intruder gained entrance to my home, and nearly my body; my humor keeps him from entering my soul.

* * *

ON FAME:
The Glittering Carrot

*My goal is to be able to say: "Fame and
fortune didn't bring me happiness!"*

I had a terrible dream last night! Mind if I share it?
(I'm the type that says: "Oh, this tastes terrible . . .
taste it!")

I dreamed that everyone in the world was declared
famous and I had just made it the hard way!

Before I knew about the declaration, I called my
mother to say:

"Mom, I have the best news! I'm finally doing the
Johnny Carson Show on the eighteenth— *Please* be
sure to watch!"

She said:

"Honey, I'd love to watch, but I'll be taping a

Griffin." Just then, Operator number six cut in with: "That'll be seventy-five cents please and don't forget to catch me on Phil Donahue."

* * *

Actually, I wouldn't mind if everyone in the world was declared famous as long as I got to be the one who told them!

* * *

ON AGING:
The Drop

Wrinkles are trophies of your experience.

I wouldn't trade my twenty-year-old complexion for
the problems that went with it . . .
   Unless, of course, I could have the complexion
without the problems . . . then, I'd take it in two
seconds!!
   I'm thirty-seven years old . . . and like I said before,
sometimes I get very annoyed with gravity . . . I
mean basically you spend twenty-five years growing up
and the next twenty-five growing down. However,
Lotus can deal with the inevitable . . . I mean in the
California Cosmic part of my mind I think, "Wow,
I've been around the sun thirty-seven times in this
body . . . that's heavy!"

But the Weinstock part thinks, "I'm thirty-seven and I've never earned enough to pay taxes."

It's a good thing my goal has always been to prove not all Jews can make money . . .

* * *

It's so important to prepare for one's senior years, so they can be met with dignity and style—à la Quentin Crisp. I just completed a course in senior citizen driving lessons. That's where they teach you:

- How to drive with the steering wheel above your head . . . and signal four blocks ahead of the turn.
- You must come to a dead stop when any other car appears on the road.
- You start perfecting the one story you plan to tell over and over for the rest of your life.

* * *

I can see my generation when we're the old folks . . . (the ones who said "Don't trust anyone over thirty") . . . in the Woodstock Convalescent Home . . . taking Lamaze death and rebirth classes . . . so laid back one of us will die, we won't know the difference . . . and right next door will be the Cocaine Convalescent Home, for people who want to die with a false sense of confidence, and be reborn with a Silver Spoon in their nose.

* * *

We don't venerate our aged like they do in some countries. I saw a documentary on a little town in the Balkans, where the average life expectancy was 163 years. You weren't even considered a person in this tribe till you were 75! The highest honor was to serve the elders.

They ate only 500 calories a day after age 50, bathed in icy streams, smoked black cigarettes, and drank a liter of vodka daily.

They interviewed the eldest on his one hundred seventy-third birthday—

"To what do you attribute your longevity?" he was asked! Well, the man couldn't answer . . . he was way too old . . . I mean he couldn't even talk . . . he was stiff . . . as a stick . . . in fact he looked so horrible he might have been dead . . . but he was respected . . . and I think that's my point.

* * *

ON FASHION:
The Vogue

If you only have one toe, you should not wear thongs!

I know it's not '80's for women to put their bodies down, but let's face it, gals, we don't all have the Jordache look. Don't get me wrong, I pride myself on being able to love women who are beautiful, but I still get annoyed at the ones who wear those short-short jogging shorts with a hint of cheek showing. I'm getting that look in long pants!

* * *

Basically I dress with the "4 C's" in mind:

- *Color*   - *Convenience*
- *Comfort*   - *Character*

I just can't see growing four-inch bloodred feline fingernails at the expense of complete incapacitation.

I mean, how do the women who sport those sculptured porcelain claws do anything for themselves? . . . button a shirt, wash a pan . . . dial a phone . . . diaper a baby . . . wipe themselves* . . . and . . . check for lumps!

Very carefully!

*Sorry, Mom.

ON COSMETICS:
The Natural Look

I think the natural look is great when you're eleven . . . or Brooke Shields (excuse me, that's redundant).

But as for me, if my smoke detector went off while I was sleeping, I'd grab my kid, my cat, and my Clinique!

ON BEAUTY:
The Peacock

. . . the skin-deep kind

Attitude speaks louder than pulchritude.

I've heard some perfect beauties (full-lipped, high-boned, satin-skinned, large-eyed, tilt-nosed types) complain that their plight as women is the hardest. That they never know if a man loves them for their beauty or their character. Now *there's* a problem I wouldn't mind handling! It's certainly better than *not* knowing if a man *doesn't* love you because you're *not* beautiful or he *doesn't* like your character.

It's not that I begrudge a beautiful woman her loveliness; it's her good karma. But some women are obnoxious with it, that is, the type who has fabulously thick hair; more hair in one section than you have on your whole head, and she loves to say things like, "You're so lucky to have hair you can see through; it's so illusive!" When she was twelve years old it was, "What I wouldn't do for acne; it's so mature." She had one blemish and it was, "Oh, I'm so broken out."

I know a lot of women who are very attractive and yet they suffer intensely on the crucifix of comparison because they're not perfect ten's. If you're gonna compare yourself, do it to a woman who's a one, not a ten. And remember, nobody else knows what you want to look like, so nobody else knows how you think you fail—

Lao Tzu summed it up when he said that in order for humanity to find one thing beautiful he thinks he must find something else ugly. Thank God we're finally living in an age where attitude speaks louder than pulchritude.

I would, however, love the convenience of natural beauty. To be the type who hops out of bed, shakes her hair, brushes her teeth, throws on jeans and a T-shirt and is ready to meet the world without a second thought. Just to wake up and take up where I left off. But, alas, I run for the rouge and the blow dryer as soon as I see the door that leads from my dreams to the puffy morning realism that awaits me in the mirror, and I remind myself that Golda Meir was my idol.

* * *

ON HEALTH FOOD:
The Virgin Molecule

Don't judge a person by what he puts into his mouth, but more by what comes out of it!

Don't take it to the extreme like I did; like I do everything. I even took moderation to an extreme. I was a total health food nut until I joined the Schick Center for the Control of Health Food Addicts. What they do to cure you is, seat you in a room filled with organic food, and every time you reach for a soybean or a sprout, they slap you with a huge piece of bacon . . . right across the face.

I was a breathtarian for a short time. They're a tribe of people who do without food altogether. They live on air. It's a very thin tribe, I might add. That's why I moved to L.A. At least the air has some meat to it.

One of the most important health discoveries is the Clay Diet. Apparently there's something about the properties in liquid clay that cleanse the toxins from your liver, which is the filter system of the body. What you do is, put powdered clay in a glass of water before you go to sleep. During the night the clay settles at the bottom and in the morning you drink the water. Not only does your liver get clean, but you start to poop* these fabulous ashtrays!

And, of course, there is the basic Water Fast. This is not only one of the best ways to detoxify, it's also a great way to get high. And water is so easy to score. A ten-day water fast is supposed to undo ten years of bad living. Be careful, though, because you can get a little weird. Around the fourth day, you get hot flashes of baked potatoes. You might find yourself putting pornographic pictures of food on the wall; little apples with lace panties, ribs in garter belts. I once dreamed I checked into a Holiday Inn with a banana split.

*Sorry, Mom.

ON JEWISH COMICS:
The Stand-up

With so many Jewish people being comics, how come Israel doesn't have a laughing wall???

ON ORGASM:
The Fickle Finger

Dear Abby:
Is it wrong to fake orgasm during masturbation?

What's the big deal about orgasm? I had one once. It was no big deal. It was April 5, 1968, 2:35 A.M., Eastern Standard Time. I had an astrological chart done on my orgasm. Turns out it was an Aries with Cancer rising, moon in Scorpio.

I'm not really sure it was an orgasm. I sneezed at that very moment, which is almost the same thing because you're not thinking when you're sneezing and you're not thinking when you're climaxing and that's the state we're really after . . . that nonthinking at-one-moment state of mind, or atonement as you Weinstocks say.

* * *

Quick quiz: Does multiple orgasm mean:

( ) A lot of people are having one?
(-) One person is having a lot?
( ) A few are having a few?

* * *

ON FOREPLAY:
The Appetizer

*Actually I prefer mental foreplay. Tell me how
wonderful my insights are, stroke my brain,
squeeze my oblongatta . . . love my lobes.*

*Bring new meaning to "you give good
head."*

ON CHILDBIRTH:
The Delivery

*Nothing will put life and sex in better perspective
than the experience of childbirth . . .*

I refer not only to the pregnant but to the
"pregnee" as well . . . More and more men are
participating in the birth of their children like they
had something to do with it . . . (It's so mid-'70's and
yet futuristic . . .) Attending classes with their wives,
they learn to time contractions and cut the umbilical
cord! . . . Brow mopping and rhythmic breathing to
the tune of "You're The Most Beautiful Gal In The
World" help make this magical event a mutually
shared experience.

My husband was so close to me during my labor . . . he was in the same city . . . I didn't really want him any closer because he's still so uptight about the natural body functions (like sleeping and eating—he considers them a sign of weakness). Had he been in the delivery room with me I would have felt I had to hold my stomach in . . .

*　*　*

ON MOTHERHOOD
The Joyous Fulfillment

Raising a child in Los Angeles is very difficult, ever since they lowered the official age of puberty to six!

There's nothing deeper than a mama's pride. Motherhood is what really liberated me. Not only did I learn the meaning of unconditional love, but I learned to respect time, balance, and the importance of nutrition when I discovered that a newborn baby *will* reject bologna and white bread.

Lili is a fabulous child, an unending joy, the result of exquisite lovemaking with my husband on April 5, 1968, 2:35 A.M., Eastern Standard Time. My daughter's much more practical than I, especially with her emotional investments, but nonetheless tolerant of my need to save anyone who thinks enough of me to ask.

Sometimes I consider her as a partner. Not quite equal. More like 60/40, or maybe 55/45, but no more than 51/49. Her way! She's a very old soul with a New Age awareness. Some of my more metaphysical friends believe her to be the reincarnation of Mme. Blavatsky, the founder of theosophy. Meanwhile, back here on earth, she pays her share of the rent by acting in TV commercials. Only products I approve; no junk foods. A brittle friend of mine once said to Lili in disbelief, "Your mother makes you pay rent?" To which she replied, "It's a great deal! I get free meals and she does the laundry."

I try so hard to be an enlightened mother. I mean, kids are such divine creatures when they arrive. The ultimate responsibility.

Oh, the doubts! The Lotus part of me rests comfortably in the knowledge that my daughter is protected in whatever she does and that she is in the One Presence and Power that guides her perfectly. But Weinstock, the JAM (Jewish American Mother) in me worries incessantly. Should I have exposed her to the *Kama Sutra* and *The Blue Lagoon* at such a tender age? Should she have accidentally eaten that hash brownie at the Summer Solstice? Then Lotus reminds Weinstock that it's better for the children to discover these things at home so they won't have to run away to find them out from someone who doesn't love them as much as we do.

Weinstock is secretly saving money for braces and a nose job; Lotus taught Lili to accept her God-given beauty as it is.

Two weeks ago Weinstock saw Lili holding her book really close while reading. Instant appointment at the

eye doctor. The doctor told Weinstock, "Your daughter holds her book close because her arms are short."
It's moments like those that cure me of my division.

* * *

DISCIPLINING CHILDREN: THE ROD

My approach is quite different from my mother's. It has to be with the children of the "Woodstock" generation. It's not the old "spare the rod" syndrome. How can you hit a kid who says, "Hey, Mom, it's your karma; you'll come back as *my* daughter!"

When my daughter was three and a half, I caught her giving birth to her doll, Lamaze. I said, "What are you doing?" She said, "Quit the questions and cut the cord."

I believe in a discipline that creates self-determination toward optimum survival, not frightened obedience just to avoid punishment. So, I've created rules my daughter wants to follow:

Examples:

1. Wherever you drop your clothes, that's exactly where they should remain!
2. When taking phone messages, do *not* write them down. If you feel you can't control yourself, write them in Sanskrit.
3. When using the last sheet of toilet paper, do *not* replace the roll.
4. Always put empty bottles and cartons back into the fridge.
5. When using Mommy's lipstick on the cat, do *not* wipe it off. Daddy finds the cat hairs hanging from Mommy's lips real attractive.
6. When using Mommy's lipstick, press real hard so

when Mommy uses it, it goes right up to her nose.

7. Changing the kitty litter is not a job for a ten-year-old; it is a job for a thirty-seven-year-old woman with back trouble.
8. When it's time to sort the laundry, flop yourself on the bed and repeat, "Why is my life so *boring?!*"
9. Whenever playing a game, if you find yourself losing, always say, "I *quit!*"
10. Don't find fault with Mommy unless at least four other adults are in the room, who can *really* help Mommy's career!
11. Don't tell Mommy that your best dress is filthy until late afternoon of that special occasion!
12. When Grandma comes for that rare visit, use as many current drug terms as possible.
13. When cleaning your room, gather all your clothes in the center of the floor and shove them directly under the bed.

Lili never breaks these rules . . . and I'm so pleased!

* * *

MOTHER'S DAY, 1968: TO MY MOTHER

Long as I remember,
I've been at odds with you,
Wishing hard to win your love
And your approval, too.
> Well, one of these days
> We're gonna see eye to eye,
> At least I'll always try.
Mama . . .
When will you bless our differences?

Dearest Mother,
It's only because you are s
so far away from home to fi
match'd the one you wove.

* *

If yo
And
It wo
To

ON LOVE:
The Flame

If Love is an Art, my husband's an abstract painter; and I'm his blue period!

There's a very popular poster which reads:
    "True Love expects nothing in return."

Show me a woman who expects nothing in return and I'll show you a woman in a coma!

* * *

Love is always there . . . it's just us who aren't.

ON ROMANCING A WOMAN:
The Game

The way to a woman's stomach is through her heart . . .

Some of my single friends tell me what's going on these days, and I'm astounded by some of the "come-ons" men are using . . . Oh, I know women use them too but those are different . . . those are "come-ins" . . . no, those are "don't come-ins."

First of all, you don't even need an approach . . . either the energy is there for love or it's not . . . but you can't tell some guys that because they've worked on their approach since puberty. To tell them they don't need it anymore is like telling a protest singer that the war is over. What do they do with their songs?

* * *

I was also shocked to hear that even in the '80's

men still discuss their sexual encounters with their friends . . . using baseball terms . . .

"Did ya score? . . .
Did you go to first? . . .
Was there some foul play? . . .
Did you slide home? . . ."

It's a game . . . It's so late '50's!

Now women, we discuss them too, in detail . . . but we use kitchen talk . . .

"Did he *ever* *burn* my cookies."
"He really *poached* my eggs."
"He was faster than minute rice . . ."
Well, you are what you eat!

Gals, when you have nothing to do one afternoon . . . look around the kitchen and see how everything relates . . .

- He opened my cabinets.
- He waxed my table.
- He braised my beef.
- He greased my griddle.
- He powdered my parsnips.
- He chilled my Chablis.

* * *

When I was still dating there was the "cool approach . . ." This was the guy with a zippo lighter that had an eight-inch flame . . . the bigger the flame, the cooler the guy . . . and he would light anything . . . your hair . . . your food . . . if you

pulled out a stick of gum the man would light it . . .
and you didn't want to embarrass him so you'd blow
gum rings . . .

Then there was the big toucher . . . he'd touch
anything the lighter would light . . . your hair . . .
your food . . . it didn't matter . . . you'd be leaving
a restaurant and as he was helping you on with your
coat his hand would accidentally brush across your
breast and you'd think "Oh, my GOD does he know
he touched me? . . ." and GOD forbid you were
wearing falsies, you didn't even know he touched
you . . .

Then there was the sympathetic approach . . . you'd
be out on a date and he'd say, "Do you mind if we
stop at my house, I have to feed my mother . . ." Just
as he pulled in the driveway and turned off the
motor, he'd rest his forehead on the steering wheel and
say, "I think I'm turning homosexual . . . if you
want, you can try and save me . . ."

Then there was the subtle approach . . . this was
the guy who you went out with to please the family
. . . the architecture major with one eyebrow and
moist palms . . . he always took you to the hottest
movie in town and during the big kiss scene, you'd
see that wet hand glistening and inching over the
armrest . . . before you knew it he was scratching
the center of your palm with his middle finger . . . in a
little circle . . .

*Wasn't that disgusting????? Was that supposed to
get us hot????*

What about the Big Surpriser . . . the guy who took
you to a drive-in . . . waited till you were totally
involved in the film . . . you'd unconsciously put your
hand in the popcorn box and there you would find

the *"big surprise"* . . . well, it wasn't always big . . .
but who's counting? . . .

* * *

I just heard about an approach to end all approaches.
The mystical occult approach. My cousin Sharon
told me about it. She met a man in Malibu who said
he reads nipples. He's an accredited Nipologist. She
went to him for a reading. He said she should get a
divorce and move into his apartment.

I scoffed at first until Sharon pointed out that there
are no two nipple prints that are the same. It's just like
fingerprints, only not as practical because most people
don't leave nipple prints at the scene of a crime!

ON CREDITS:
The Admiration Particle

*Lotus thinks the glory or credit belongs
to GOD. We just channel GOD's ideas!
Weinstock wants the credit for everything
good that happens in the neighborhood! I
wish I didn't care who knew!*

There's a part of me that just hates it when I'm at a
dinner party and I think of something witty to add to
the conversation, but because I'm not completely
confident in the degree of its cleverness, I say it softly
to the person sitting next to me. She has more
certainty on the remark than I do, so she says it loud
enough for everyone to hear, and gets a huge laugh!
It's the hit remark of the evening! . . . then at the
peak of the laugh, she says softly "Lotus said that . . ."
of course, no one hears that part but me.

Weinstock seethes and wants to shout . . . "I *said it first,*" but fears looking as small as the woman is, for not giving the credit where it's due. Lotus sips wine, and is grateful for the opportunity to make someone else popular!

* * *

Do you suppose Matthew, Mark, Luke, and John fought over credit . . . billing, and whose premise it was first . . .

MATTHEW: I thought of the Resurrection . . . and the Temptation.

MARK: Yeah, well I brought the hooker into it . . . it was me who made it commercial.

LUKE: Yeah, well I gave Jesus some balls . . . a little aggression . . . anger in the Temple . . . anger's a very popular emotion . . . you had him written really fey.

JOHN: Yeah, well I liked Him better the other way. He was holier . . . more laid back. I was more comfortable with Him!

LUKE: The general public has to identify a little . . . As it is we're asking them to buy a helluva story.

* * *

We all want the credit though—don't we? Even the Bible thumpers want credit with GOD for the souls they save . . . Well, just like the Bible says . . . "all is vanity and vexation" . . . (Ecclesiastes)

It's amazing how you can get an ego about having no ego.

* * *

59

ON THE BIBLE:
The Blueprint

Even if you don't believe a word of the Bible, you've got to respect the person who typed all that! . . .

What a commitment! Something major was compelling the author;

I can't even type a three-page outline.

ON RELIGION:
The Crutch

Religion is the opposite of negligence.

Dear Reader,

Today was a rough one— I've been feeling like a wishbone in the hands of Self-Love and Self-Hate— for being so disorganized . . . (my life is like a messy purse). Not only do I want credit, but I want some discipline . . . especially because I fathom myself a disciple . . . of what I'm not certain, but I definitely got the "call," however weak the connection . . .

I could hear GOD's voice on the other end of the cosmic phone—(an unlisted number) and I said, "I just read in the paper that you were dead," and He told me that it made good copy but that in truth He was extremely tired because people don't leave Him alone for two seconds.

... *"It's constantly 'gimme this and gimme that ...
I want a shag rug, a CB radio ... a tape deck ...
gimme a Beta-Max ... and a best-seller!'"*

*Then He started crying, "Leave Me alone for
GOD's sake ... the only people I even like anymore
are the atheists because they play hard to get and
the people who flash on Me with the occasional toke,
because when they see Me they don't ask for
anything, they are just so glad to see Me ... The most
they impose on Me is a simple, 'Hey, what's happen-
ing' ... they don't even want an answer. The people
who really annoy the Hell out of Me are the ones
who stand on their heads for hours, breathing crazily to
get My attention ... 'Look at me ... Look at me'
... and I hate that cheap vanilla incense ..."*

* * *

*I've always been a seeker, in search of the path that
would make me feel the least guilty about who I am.
In fact I nearly killed myself in the '70's looking for
eternal life ... a junkie for "peak experiences" aka
GOD consciousness.*

*I took Est (that's where nine thousand people
crowd into a room the size of the one you're sitting in,
looking for their space ...) By the way, you'll be
thrilled to know that Evelyn Wood has a speedy Est
course now. You can find out you're an asshole in
two and a half minutes (a real time-saver for the '80's).*

*Then I took a course called Pest—that's where you
pester yourself into being an honest person. You get a
little Jewish Jiminy Cricket by the name of Elaine
Pincus who sits on your shoulder and constantly says,
"Be yourself, be yourself."*

Scream Therapy was a real hoot! — That's where

you scream your guts out to get to the heart of your problems—which in my case became nodes in my throat.

When I was into Dream Therapy, I dreamed that Woody Allen was GOD and that in two thousand years we'd all be driving around with an analyst's couch on our dashboards.

In Hypno Therapy I was regressed to my original trauma. The damaging event of this life . . . my birth . . . When the doctor slapped my tush. Under hypnosis I could actually see his face . . . he was so hostile . . . saying things like, "I hate kids . . . Who needs 'em?" In that moment I knew if I could find that doctor and slap his tush, I would find me.

So I went to Philadelphia and found him in an old age home on his deathbed and asked, "Doctor Grossman, would you like to clean up your karma? I mean don't you think it's fair if you slapped me on the way in, I should slap you on the way out?"

Kundalini Yoga was very powerful, but quite honestly I never knew if my kundalini was rising or I had gas.

Then there was Subud . . . Zen Buddhism . . . TM . . . and FM . . . I read the handbook to higher consciousness . . . The footbook to other realms.

Don't get me wrong, please. I'm not putting any of these spiritual excursions down 'cause from each one I got a very valuable technique for getting more in touch with myself—

From 1974 to 1977 I would wake up every morning and stand on my head for twenty minutes . . . then a half hour of joy breathing . . . followed by a lengthy but melodic salutation to the angels of the air, earth, fire, and water—

I contemplated the feeling of one-leg jogging.

*I said hello to the sun in twenty languages . . .
good-bye to the moon in ten—*

*I was filled with the light and I felt divine— The only
problem was by the time I finished morning meditation it was 9 o'clock at night and it was time for
evening meditation.*

*The most guileless woman I know took me to a Born
Again meeting not long ago . . . and I have to be
honest. I was Born Again! But I died on the way home.
I had the worst fight with my husband . . . over
which was the true path to salvation.*

*In desperation I fell to my knees and called out to
GOD, "I'm so confused . . . Please tell me your real
name so when I pray I know you'll hear me."*

And GOD said,

> *"Well, you can call me Jesus*
> *and you can call me Buddha*
> *and you can say Jehovah . . .*
> *. . . but please call and I will get back to you."*

* * *

*I'll never forget my first peyote trip when I got the
call from GOD to be the New Messiah—or should I say
Ms. Siah. Yes, me—I was his new Favorite and I ran
into the bathroom to catch a glimpse of His chosen
one in the mirror and there she was with a straight-
haired wig and falsies. When I came down I realized if I
were supposed to be the only one, my mother
probably would have told me.*

* * *

*But in the '80's I have a more casual relationship
with GOD.*

Like no heavy commitments . . . OK.

*Like we still live together and we still love each
other but GOD's seeing other people and so am I.*

ON WOMEN IN COMEDY:
The Femme To Fool

*In the '80's I predict women will be more
concerned with developing their sense of
humor than their breasts. It makes more
sense. Your humor doesn't sag after
childbirth.*

In fact, it gets better. I have seen the most solemn
women become inordinately playful in the presence
of a baby. Completely stripped of all inhibitions, they
take comedic risks that make Carol Burnett look like
Nancy Reagan. They'll grab a baby's tush and squeal,
"Who's is this? How big is this? Sooo big."
   If we could only remember that inside every human
being there is still a baby waiting to be gitchy gitchy
gooed, we'd never find ourselves in a situation we
couldn't handle.

You hear about all the sexual harrassment on the job. Say you're at the office. It's 5:12 P.M. Everyone's gone home but you and the boss and he's coming on to you in such a way that you know your job's in jeopardy if you don't give him what he wants. Well, find the baby in the boss. Grab his you-know-what, and say, in a high-pitched voice, "Who's is this? How big is this? Soooo big!" He'll stop harassing you! However, he might want to breast-feed.

* * *

ON JOHNNY CARSON:
The Comic's Dream

He's the Dalai-Lama of comedy. A veritable pillar of cuteness. It's no accident that his initials are J. C.

Last night I dreamed I did the *Tonight Show* and I killed, but Richard Dawson was hosting.

After the show I phoned my mom for those long-awaited words of praise.

"Hello, Mom," I said. "What did you think?" She said: "Honey, you know how I feel about Johnny—when he's not on I just don't watch."

* * *

ON JEALOUSY:
The Worst Emotion

*Cruel jealousy—this heart isn't big enough
for both of us.*

To me, jealousy is the cancer of emotions. It's the
pain and shame of separateness that occurs when you
actually think someone else is better than you are,
especially when your lover and/or husband is looking
at her through the eyes of his pee pee.

I have learned to deal with it thusly!

Say you're at a party and a beautiful woman walks
in with legs up to her neck. She's the type who buys a
pants suit and doesn't need the jacket. Well, I point
her out to my husband immediately . . . "Honey, isn't
she gorgeous?" You see, if you discover her, *first*, he
can't be Columbus. Columbus will explore her and
settle there.

If that should backfire because he's aware of this trick or he remembers that Columbus didn't actually discover America first, throw yourself on the floor, grab his ankle and scream—

"Don't leave me, my father has money!"

It will at least get him to leave the party before he can stake claim!

I used to think that women were the more jealous sex. *Not true* . . . It just manifests itself differently. My husband's into nonspecific jealousy. He's very territorial. If he weren't so elegant I swear he'd shit in the corner to let another man know who didn't live at my house . . . I loved his jealousy up to the point where I found him reading an old potion book written thousands of years ago by men who wanted to keep their women chaste . . . One of the potions actually read . . . "Take the privy members of a wolf, and the hairs from under his chin and put them in her drink when she knoweth not . . . and she will never cheat on you . . ." She will also never drink again . . . *Imagine* finding wolf hairs in your wine . . .

* * *

Dear Abby:

My husband's becoming very successful and he's not trying so hard to be the cause in my universe anymore.* There was a time when I couldn't slice a carrot without him invalidating me by showing me a better angle. Now he doesn't even notice. Does that mean he loves me less?

He has a new female employee who he now treats as poorly as he used to treat me . . . It hurts. I overheard him call her an idiot once and my heart

*Boss me around.

nearly stopped. When I confronted him with the fact that he was now being as rude to her as he used to be to me, he said, "Don't be silly, honey, I'd never treat anyone as poorly as I treat you."

Should I believe him?

*   *   *

ON CANCER:
The Dread Dis-ease

A great way to beat Cancer is to die for a cause . . . It doesn't even matter what your cause is . . .

This year my cause is Immortality.

Last year, it was to get real parsley back into Denny's. It's the only thing I ate in those restaurants when I was totally organic . . . Now they make it in Japan.

In fact, I used to be a member of "Parsley Growers of America." We would meet once a month and picket outside Howard Johnson's and Denny's . . . then afterward we'd sit down to a fabulous meal of a huge sprig of parsley and a little garni of meat and potatoes . . .

* * *

Another way to beat the number two *dis-ease,* is to laugh at it . . . Laughter is one of the strongest medicines on the planet! . . . Call me kooky . . . call me Norman Cousins, but if laughter is strong enough to kill an orgasm . . . surely it's strong enough to kill cancer!

So if you find a little lump that doesn't belong, just tell it a joke . . . *humor* and *tumor* . . . they rhyme for a reason! . . . (remember there are no accidents in this Universe) . . . Here's a great joke to tell your lump . . .

"Why did the moron throw the cat in the washing machine?"

—"He was a moron!"

Now you may not get a total remission from this joke but it's a great place to start . . . Start small . . . try it on a hive!

Of course there's the Wheatgrass Cure . . . and the Clay Diet . . . and vitamin C . . . and many new alternatives which I can't get into right now because it's time to check for lumps . . .

* * *

ON PSYCHIC PHENOMENA:
The Bent Spoon

I belong to an ESP group. We never meet, though. We already know what the meetings are going to be about.

We've only just begun to tap the power of our minds— Uri Geller is a perfect example. Remember Uri from the Enquirer? He's the man who can bend spoons with psychic energy. He can look at a normal spoon and without touching it, make it bend.

Isn't that a testimony to the unlimited resource we've all been given to work with . . . he's got disciples all over the world . . . Now people are bending spoons in Sicily . . . chopsticks in China . . .

But I think if you've realized this kind of power, why bend a bloody spoon? Do something useful . . . clear a slum!

I don't want to make a value judgment on Uri because he is an extraordinary man, and besides he's already suffering a setback—

A woman just slapped a child support suit on him. She claims he bent her IUD.

Did you know . . .

There are Yogis on this planet who really *can* walk through walls?? After years and years of deep concentration, they can physically duplicate the molecular structure of a wall in such a way that they are able to dissolve themselves through the wall to the other side.

But why??? We have doorways now!

* * *

ON THE WOMAN'S MOVEMENT:
The De-liberation

*I'm very dependent upon my husband for
my independence!*

Aren't we liberated and aren't we lonely?

Guys, please catch up. Only teasing. No, I'm not.
Yes, I am. No, I'm not. Yes, I . . .

Women's liberation! How far are we gonna take it?
What is our place in the divine plan? How self-
determined can a woman get before "they" call her
a dike?

How much can a man cry before "they" call him a
fag?

The answers, my friend, are blowin' in the wind
. . . somewhere at Hollywood and Vine.

November 1979 headline in *The Enquirer* read,

"Women Can Have Babies Without Men." They actually stated all you needed was two eggs and no sausage. I can see the commandment, "Honor thy mother and thy mother."

Please, may the difference never die. God knows the difference between the . . .

- static and the ec/static moments
- the ease and the dis/eased moments
- the fused and the con/fused
- the promise and the com/promised
- the takes and the mis/takes
- the liberated and the de/liberated
- the pulsed and the re/pulsed
- the passion and the com/passion (the sweetest of the passions) . . .

* * *

Yet there are moments in my relationship with my husband when the man is so insensitive to woman's plight, when he questions my contribution in such a way I wish I had a pill for him that would induce a state exactly like labor. Just for five minutes. I'm not talking a heavy . . . 'venge trip;

I happen to adore him.

* * *

But sometimes he so lacks compassion, that I feel a five-minute experience in labor would do wonders for his soul: feet in stirrups, screaming, "Oh, God," and a doctor coming toward him with shoe trees, *fresh from the fridge,* saying, "Relax, it will just be another thirty-two hours."

Guys, that's really not as bad as it sounds. Actually there's nothing I'd rather do than relax with a pair of shoe trees in me, mint julep in one hand, discussing international law.

*   *   *

While we're on the subject of liberated women, I think Brenda Vaccaro deserves some admiration particles. She had a lot of "eggs" to come out for tampons after the toxic shock scare. When I heard that news, I went into shock. I knew then that the FDA didn't care about women. If they did, they would have known to test those tampons on rats.

*   *   *

By the way, I use the term "eggs" instead of balls. I think it's inappropriate for a woman to use the term balls to define courage. We should be able to look at women like Sandra O'Connor and say, "Man she's got such ovum."

*   *   *

ON ANGER:
The Popular Emotion

Anger is fear with an escape clause.

ON REINCARNATION:
The Next Time Around

*I don't think the concept of reincarnation is
any more phenomenal than life itself . . .
but why is it that you never meet anyone who
wasn't famous in their last life?*

I have met Cleopatra thirty-seven times.
You never meet a seamstress or a plumber!
Last night I went to a "Stop The Nukes" vegetarian barbecue, and there were three Beethovens waiting
in line for a second helping of vega-ribs.

*   *   *

Ever since I experienced the death of a true loved
one, I have been comforted only by the Lotus thought
that there is life after death and that he's been with
me, on another plane, watching over my every move.

But then Weinstock thinks, oh my GOD, what if he *has* been watching me all these years and he's seen me pick my nose—how embarrassing.

* * *

ON MARIJUANA:
The Sacred Herb

It's so '60's and yet somehow timeless.

It's very difficult to be a dope-smoking mother! Much as I enjoy the occasional toke (music is sweeter, insights are richer), the last time I had a toke of good Columbian on Laundry Day, it took me six hours to sort two pairs of white identical socks!

* * *

I do, however, think it would be saner were grass to be legalized . . . if only to remove the "Paranoia" factor. Just in case you find you're the only one "wrecked" in a social situation, you don't have to try to pretend you're normal . . . Nothing will screw you up faster than trying to figure out what another paranoid person thinks "normal" is.

But let's be sane about the legalization . . . let's not do it in a way where the Russians can say . . . "Now we got 'em."

*   *   *

It should not be available for everyone— Marijuana is a *yin* herb—(expansive—while tobacco is *yang*— (contracting)—different tokes for different folks! (Lotus smokes pot, Weinstock smokes Camel Lights).

*   *   *

When ninety million Americans admit they smoke it, and it's finally legal, the Sobriety Test will be if you can remember you're looking for your license . . . you're cool.

*   *   *

YOU'LL BE THRILLED TO KNOW THAT GRASS IS SANCTIONED IN THE BIBLE

Genesis I, Verse 11 . . . and God said . . .

"let the Earth bring forth grass
. . . the herb yielding seed
and He saw that it was good."

What do you think the "burning bush" really was? It could have been low-grade Mexican; he was on a mountain, you need less. The reason they didn't make it more obvious in the Bible is because it wasn't popular, since they had no snacks in those days. You never once hear mention of a glazed doughnut throughout the entire book and when you have the munchies (low blood sugar desires) you don't want to eat a fish or a loaf of bread . . . you want Sara Lee!

Let's set the scene . . .

You're sitting around the table with a few friends
. . . you smoked three joints of the best Oregon
Homegrown three hours ago . . . you've "rapped"
about the entire universe, your mouth is now sticking
to your teeth; you have fur on your tongue and you
want coffee *Haägen Dazs* more than life itself . . .
but your host walks in with a cod fish . . .

It's not going to be popular!

* * *

Imagine how Moses must have felt when he got to
the top of Sinai and he saw a bush that was burning . . .
In front, he was exhausted and irritable . . . (have
you ever tried to climb a mountain in flimsy sandals?)
Naturally, his first instinct was to blow out the
"bush," but on the inhale he got totally wrecked . . .
And then the dialogue with GOD—
"Oh my God . . . Vat a beautiful flem!
Vat an inspeeration!
It makes me vant to write ten tings!"

* * *

Surely in your life you've gotten so stoned on one
thing or another that you thought you could write the
laws for all humanity. That state of mind where all
the pieces fit and you have peace at last. Well that's
what peace is . . . the plural of pieces . . . where
you can view your life experiences from the point
where it all makes perfect sense . . . when you can
finally say things like:

*Oh, that's why I was born in Philadelphia so I
could learn the meaning of brotherly love and rock
'n roll . . . and that's why I had to go to Camp*

*Indian Trails, against my will, so Susan Ginsberg
could turn me on to Kahlil Gibran . . . in the
'50's . . . which prepared me for the "Paradigm
Shift" in the '60's . . . and a husband in the
'70's—who wanted to live five blocks away . . .**

Of course, if all those things hadn't happened to
me I wouldn't be here right now where "It's later than
it's ever been."

* * *

Wouldn't it be great if while you were having one of
those moments of clarity, you could write down a
little phrase that would encapsulate the whole experience and you'd never have to get "stoned" again.
You'd just read the phrase and plug in to infinite
intelligence.

Well it happened to me once. It was my good karma
to have a pencil with me while I was flashing, and I
wrote down two words which sum up the universal
experience . . .

"everything's everything"

Lotus knows that's true . . . Weinstock says "but
it's not that helpful."

*See Gibran's "Teaching on Marriage" in *The Prophet*.

ON DIET PILLS:
The Fast Lane

I loved having the edge on life—

I had a one-a-day Eskatrol diet pill habit from 1965 to 1967 . . . *El dangeroso* . . .

Prescription of course . . . but

I lied to myself like most "peak freaks" do.

I told myself I was taking them to lose weight but I just wound up eating faster!

I spoke only in rhyme and my house was arranged in alphabetical order . . . armchairs, bed, couch, dresser, and end tables.

* * *

ON DEATH:
The Last Gasp

Don't take me yet Lord,
I'm not finished being afraid to die.

If life is a picture with infinite exposure
Is death the darkroom,
closed shutter
the negative
blowup? . . .

DEATH IS THE GREAT EQUALIZER

It kinda dwarfs the importance of a broken fingernail
or the fact that you don't climax every time you
make love— Makes me think twice about wasting time!
I figure if I was on my deathbed with eighteen

minutes left to live, and I thought back about some of the ways I've wasted my time, I'd get really annoyed!

1. I've wasted at least twelve hours of my life looking for a better parking space. I want them back!
2. A whole summer wishing I were black.
3. Six years wishing I could at least sing black.
4. Two years lamenting the time I've wasted thinking about the time I've wasted.
5. Four hours watching *Love Boat* reruns.
6. Ten minutes vacuuming (a little joke for you sloths).

* * *

THE WEINSTOCK TIME-SAVERS

I think we fear death mostly because we think we won't get a chance to live out all our fantasies—so I've come up with some time-savers for you:

1. Eat over the sink (serve the entire family over the sink) . . . one pot . . . one spoon . . . and if you're really pressed for time, eat right on the toilet!
2. Floss and Drive—tie one end to the steering wheel, hook your teeth over and look for U-turns! You get those wisdom teeth!!
3. If you're thinking of having a child, why not adopt a grownup. Preferably one who drives and does housework.
4. For you advanced dope smokers who spend three hours a day looking for your keys, try the fabulous new fingernail shaped exactly like your door key. (Available at any head shop). You'll never have to look for your keys again, they'll always be right at your fingertips.

5. Here's a real time-saver for you married couples: My husband and I have learned to economize in our communication! We both talk at the same time! In fact, we've gotten it down to two words: *"You're interrupting."*

6. As soon as you get your paycheck, throw it directly down the drain.

7. Put cancer right in your food.

8. Swim with your laundry.

9. Guys, when you're kissing a woman for the first time, *please* don't shove your tongue directly down her throat. It's such an invasion, it'll take you months to get her hot again! Sip your pleasures and make kissing a mutually shared experience.

or

Eliminate foreplay completely. This way, you'll have more time afterwards in which to discuss how unfulfilling your sexual relationship is.

10. When starting analysis, admit to the following problems in your first session:

a. You hated your mother.

b. You fear latent homosexuality.

c. You doubt your ability to ever be truly happily married.

d. You have difficulty believing in a GOD who would allow small children to die.

11. If you absolutely have to have real plants in your home, buy cactus. They only have to be watered once a month, and even if they die, who could tell from the way they look!

12. And the biggest time-saver of all—*TELL THE TRUTH!*

* * *

Tell the truth—

* * *

Lotus knows that life is eternal—that "death" is just a doorway to a different dimension—

Weinstock doesn't know for sure what waits for us beyond this door—she only knows that "hugs" don't happen anymore and that makes her a basket case on the subject of losing a loved one!

* * *

ON MASOCHISM:
The Leather Rule

Do unto others exactly the opposite as you'd have them do unto you.

ON ULCERS:
The Ultimate Surrender

Stop eating your heart out—
It's too hard to stomach.

At one point on my path of surrender to the greater me, my image of The Perfect Spiritual Gal was one who softly spoke only two phrases to her man:

"You're right."

"I'm sorry."

And three to her child:

"You're perfect."

"I love you."

"There, there."

All bitter pills were to be swallowed in solitude—

I was well on my way to becoming pure Lotus, when Weinstock got an ulcer.

Too much surrender—

I even allowed my food to eat me—

ON BAD KARMA:
The Cause and Defect

The ultimate in bad karma is when you have to come back as yourself

ON ABORTION:
The Lesser of Two Evils

*Don't have a baby unless you're willing to
be born again along with it.*

If the point of conception is the beginning of life, that
means anything that interferes with that moment is a
form of murder.

For example, a woman would be committing a crime
if she wore an unattractive hat or talked loudly . . .
during . . .

I think the abortion law should be extended to
chickens as well.

I happen to know a couple of chickens who've
been cooped up for years . . . bare webbed and
pregnant . . . no matter how much they squawk,
they're forced to make babies . . . doomed to play the

role of mother hen—and for what? . . . chicken feed!

(Very Weinstock)

* * *

ON PREJUDICE:
The Narrow Mind

My one prejudice is hating prejudiced people.

If we must keep prejudice in this earthly game, for the
sake of the economy—let's pick on people who
never had acne . . .

I'm bored by racial delineation . . . bored and hurt
. . . the KKK are buying more sheets than ever;
anti-Semitism is on the rise; and more and more I'm
seeing black men out with black women . . . I think it
was *Roots II* that made the difference . . . now I
hear they're making the gay version of *Roots* . . . it's
going to be a very short film . . . because they can
only trace the roots back one generation.

* * *

I always pray when there's a violent crime in the

news, that the criminal is not from a minority group
. . . We can't afford to make those kinds of mistakes
. . . I know how I felt in the summer of '77 when
they caught the "Son of Sam" and his name was
David Berkowitz . . . I think every Jew in America
was thinking the same thing . . .

David Berkowitz . . . What a strange name for a
Puerto Rican!

Then we found out he was adopted . . . We were
on the phone . . .

"Hello, Bea . . . he's adopted."

* * *

ON NEW AGE PREJUDICE:
The New Narrow Mind

Macrobiotics versus The Mucousless Diet System

"Hello, Celestial, have you seen Aura lately? She's so *yin* . . . so *san paku* . . . I mean she's got an eighth of an inch of white showing under her eyeballs. She may say she's a total fruitarian, but I have seen several Heath Bar wrappers at the bottom of her purse . . ."

* * *

Why start a movement if it's only to move the hate from one side to the other?

ON JUDGMENT:
The Immoral Majority

Please don't judge me on the breaks I've had, but rather on the way in which I've mended them.

It says in the Bible: "Judge not that ye be not judged." To me that means if you're busy judging someone you're not busy loving them . . . and you're only as good as the love you experience. Everytime I judge someone, within five minutes I realize it's a clue to one of my own shortcomings . . .

* * *

I look at someone like Anita Bryant for short periods (very short) and I wonder what compelled her to judge a group of people who chose a different path than she did, when it was probably a woman like

Anita that made some men gay in the first place . . . I don't think we realize how much time we spend making superficial judgments on each other, that limit our experience:

For example: Do you judge the person next to you in the supermarket by the groceries he has (which is why shopping feels like a chore, because you never feel love at the market?). I admit I do it occasionally. I don't know why, but I judge people who buy beef jerky . . . and once I was standing next to a woman who had six cans of Alpo dog food and hamburger helper and she was screaming at her kid, *"Sit Billy!"* and I judged her . . . "Oh my GOD what is she feeding her kid?"

And how about the kind of judgment you experience in the Express Lane . . . when you have eleven items??? . . . You can feel the hate vibes building up on your back . . . Once the man standing behind me took the rubber divider and slapped it down on my eleventh item . . . which was butter . . .

* * *

Do you judge someone with a stain on his shirt? What is a stain? . . . it's dirt! . . . just matter in the wrong place . . . there might be a fabulous person behind that dirt and you'll never notice, just because of a few misplaced molecules! Sure you go to someone's house and you find a dirty dish in their sink . . . you'll accept it. If you find a dirty dish in their bed, you cross them out of your phone book.

Isn't it amazing where we draw the line— Find fur on someone's cat— OK. Find fur on their strawberries— exclude them from your prayers.

Do you judge people who cross their sevens (7) to prove they've been to Europe?

How about the gal who flosses with a strand of hair,
or,
the man in the blue polyester?
blondes who use the word "karma" a lot?

* * *

ON WORLD PEACE
The Missing Piece

*Let's declare the new Promised Land as a
State of Mind . . . Then everyone can live
there!*

World peace will only be possible when Self-Love is
considered a virtue!
   It says in the Bible:
   "Love your neighbor as you love yourself."
   If you hate yourself, your neighbor's in trouble!

* * *

   World peace might be boring but I'd like about a
thousand years to find out . . . The first step toward it
should be to change all news programs so they only
report the *good* news . . .

• 3.1 billion people were not robbed or raped today.

- 1.6 million people made love for the first time.
- 300 couples climaxed together and nearly everyone said they'd be willing to try it again.
- Katie McMann finished the third day of her juice fast with very little anxiety . . . She said her psoriasis is clearing up for the first time in six years and she needs a lot less sleep.

* * *

ON WORLD LEADERS:
The Big Dealers

I think all world leaders should live together either in
the Smithsonian Institute or in a commune on a
nuclear testing site. Whatever they can grow there they
can eat.

Twice a year they must participate in the birth of a
baby, preferably during winter and summer solstice.

Every New Year's Eve, after a three-day juice fast,
they'll go to the desert to ingest the Magic Mushroom
and read Seth Speaks, Carlos Casteneda, Sam Pisar,
and Lenny Bruce. While playing a tape of Johann
Pachelbel's Canon in D Major, they can make a joint
New Year's resolution.

In case this comes to pass in my daughter's lifetime, I
have left instructions for her to volunteer for the
cleanup and massage committee.

ON GUN CONTROL:
The Bullet Proof

*Forget about controlling hand guns. It's too late! One out of four people already own a gun.
The only solution is to legalize marijuana so everyone will forget where they hid the ammunition!*

ON FIDELITY:
The Bed and Bored

*Beware of men who say they are separated
from their wives—they usually mean since
breakfast.*

*If man is basically a polygamist . . .
woman is basically a harem all of her own . . .
marry a man who recognizes all the women
in you.*

ON INNER STRENGTH:
The Will

The will is like a muscle and it's got to be exercised!

In Hollywood, Self-Will is the art of pretending your destiny was your choice.

You can't always have what you want, but you can always want what you have, so a true exercise of will is learning to love what you have to do.
. . . Pass the Brillo, please!

ON FEMALE ADOLESCENCE:
The Raging Hormone

*I grew up thinking GOD gave you breasts to
make you popular!*

I remember when I was in the seventh grade . . .
you had one of two rumors passed around about you
. . . either you wore falsies or you were a whore
. . . and if you wore falsies you wanted desperately to
be considered a whore but your mother always said
. . . "Don't worry, whores don't get married . . ."
So for five years I wore my falsies knowing someday
I could exchange them for a bridal hanky . . . and
then I was seventeen years old—and I turned around
and all the whores were getting married—

* * *

My daughter's entering adolescence . . . a term she

claims adults created when they ceased to understand their kids . . . Since we share everything I'm
going through it with her . . . This time I'm gonna
get it right!

* * *

I taught my daughter what Lenny Bruce said, "If
there's anything dirty about the body, the fault lies
with the manufacturer."
I wish I'd known that when I was in my teens—
I've wasted half my life hiding the facts of the other
half of my life—hormone Hell . . . oh, the pain and
shame of separateness.

* * *

Do you remember when you were thirteen and on
the beach, and it was that time of the month? . . .
and you would have died if anyone found out . . .
remember? . . . well forget it . . . *They all knew*
. . . of course, they were all swimming in the ocean
. . . you were knitting on the sand . . . What else
could it mean? . . . then someone would get the idea
to throw you in . . . to be cute . . . That was humor
in those days . . . "Let's throw her in. She's got her
period. . . ." Do you remember the horror of being
in the ocean and not knowing whether you should look
for sharks or swim to Europe? . . .

* * *

108

ON SUCCESS:
The Big Win

Success is a journey—not a destination.

Oh, if only Weinstock could remember that!

ON HUNGER:
The Empty Plate

If there's one hungry person, it's a hungry world!

When I leave my body I'm donating my fat to the Third World!

ON WINNING:
The Competition

*My goal is to be the most noncompetitive
person in the world . . .*

I thought when I became a mother the competition
would cease . . . Little did I know how much my
daughter's Caesarean birth would be looked down
upon by all the Le Buoyans and the Lamazians . . .
Little did I know how much class distinction would
exist between the cloth diaper set and the Pampers
users! . . . Little did *I want* to know of all the calls
that came in with the morning sun, about whose baby
slept through the night, because my kid was a night
person just like her mom . . . I didn't give up a
promising career just to enter my daughter in a race
of motor control . . . All I cared about after I'd
counted my daughter's fingers and toes and was

certain she could see and hear . . . was that she'd
enjoy her infancy and grow up to be a genius . . .

I wasn't gonna lay any heavy demands on her like
crawl before anyone else's kid, . . . as long as she
knew the alphabet by her first birthday . . .

I hate competing . . . if I win, I feel guilty about
the loser . . . and if I lose I check for lumps to cheer
me up.

Lotus reminds Weinstock that there's no such thing
as losing: "All stumbling blocks are inverted stepping
stones."

* * *

THE LOTUS POSITION:
To The Child In Everyone

Find Comfort
     in your diary
my child
    and with your other hand,
applaud
    the drone
for what you understand
    to be your agony today,
Tomorrow, shall be of a
    willful tone

Find Comfort
    in your daily walk

my child
    and say hello to
things you've never known
    and lift yourself
to touch their hands
    and love them,
for all time,
For soon again, you'll have to walk alone

Find Comfort
    in your looking glass
my child
    and with reflections
Altered,
    by your eyes,
Kneel down
    before the
Bible of Your Consciousness,
    Replacing all the needs
that sought disguise

Find Comfort
    in your loneliness
my child
    for only you have seen
what it could see
    and no one other than yourself
is friends with what you fear
    you'll fail
in search of what you thought you'd
    like to be

Find Comfort
    in your solitude
my child

114

while all those words like
"lonely" disappear
        for though you've been
betrothed
        you've clothed her royally
in thought
        with tarnished prayer
and questions bent by fear

Find Comfort
        in the wordless world
my child
        and love the "tickless time"
you've never known
        and generously

Divinity
        will give till it's

Infinity
        and

You
        shall find you've never
been alone

Find Comfort
        in the words you read
my child
        They are only here, for you
to understand,
        that you are not
the only
child with a diary,
        and

the road to GOD
belongs to *Everyman* . . .
Be not afraid to take this road
my child
    · or you'll someday find
that you're in someone's
        way
and though the plight seems toilsome,
        please think again, "cause"
We all must come
The
        Sun
Reminds the
        Morning, every day!
Be not afraid, to
        Love
The
        Rain
my child
        Its purpose is
as
        Godly
as the sun,
        and *look*
to all of
        Nature's lessons
everytime you feel
        confused
and
        you shall find
We all are here as
        one.

            . . . Lotus

            * * *

Always remember wherever you go and whatever you do that:

Angels can fly because they take themselves lightly.

—Ram Dass

ON ENDINGS:
The Last Page

To Every Position There's an Opposition

Dearest Dearest Reader: It's later than it's ever been.

I feel one hundred forty-four pages closer to you and I'm delighted by it all. It's as though I've had lunch with the world.

Let's stay in touch. If you've figured out my purpose—please fill in the form on the facing page and send it back to me— I'm looking forward to finding out just what it is.

. . . Weinstock

c/o Dana/Corwin Ent.
2029 Century Park East
Los Angeles, CA 90067

Dear Lotus,
     Weinstock,

              (pick one or both)

To me your purpose is _____

_____

_____

_____

_____

_____

_____

_____

_____

_____

and I love you.

_____
Signature

_____

_____
Address

THANKS

Lotus would like to acknowledge everyone in the world for just simply being.

Weinstock would like to give large heartfelt thanks to Bill Dana, for his all-around wonderfulness, and for thinking my funny could make me some money; Stan Corwin, for his clarity, and the ability to translate it into confusing terms so I could understand; Evy Dana, for showing me the virtue in being more demanding; Shelley Weinstock, for being very Weinstock when I was too Lotus; Norman Klein, for illuminating my contemplating; Meg Staahl, for the icing—what's a cake without it?

And for (bio) feedback, and typing, thanks to Don Goldberg, Albert Crane, Vinny Sorrentino, Phyllis Carlyle, James Weinstock and Cori Bishop.

Overdue Thanks

To Roy Silver, for giving me a ticket to ride on the Show Biz Train; Bud Prager, for my berth; Mitzi Shore, for knowing "my time" would come; Richie Havens, for giving me my wings; Marsha and Hal Goldstein and Jim Baker for a place to land; L. Ron Hubbard, for a sane definition of sanity . . .

And my one of a kind mother, Lucy Berger, for her keen sense of humor and romance; and Martin for his shining example; Bennett, for showing me it's okay to be successful at something you love to do; and my darling daughter Lily for the constant reminder that even when I hated every word I'd written, I was lucky to have a deal; and to my extraordinary husband, David, for being an endless source of material.

And of course, to my wonderful friends I say, if you think you should have been thanked personally, please write your name on the line below.

Thanks to _____.

I want to thank my husband* for not listening to my insights . . . or I would never have been forced to write them down . . .

*Whom I love dearly (that's for you, honey).

ABOUT THE AUTHOR

Lotus wrote her first song at age 10: "What Good Are Memories?" At age 11, she wrote the sequel: "No Good Unless They're Funny." Born in Philadelphia on January 29, 1943, before being an Aquarian was song-worthy, Lotus (then Marlena) justified her existence by writing intense poetry and song, and studying dance at the Philadelphia Dance Academy of Music.

After attending Emerson College in Boston as a Theatre Arts major, it was clear to Lotus that her legs were too short to pursue dance any further, and that comedy was her winning ticket. She joined a musical-comedy repertory company, playing the ingenue soubrette leads in over thirty musicals ranging from *West Side Story* to *Gypsy.*

After moving to New York where she studied dance at June Taylor's (hoping her legs would grow again) and acting with Wynn Handman, founder of the American Place Theatre, Lotus took a job as a hostess at The Bitter End where Woody Allen and Bill Cosby were getting their acts together. Cosby's manager spotted her and made her part of a comedy duo known as The Turtles, which toured the national club circuit.

Embarking on a solo career as a stand-up comedienne, Miss Weinstock, then Maurey Haydn, opened for folk stars Phil Ochs, John White, Tim Hardin and Richie Havens, who later recorded her songs. It was in L.A. that Miss Weinstock met Lenny Bruce who taught her the art of comedy that makes people think as well as laugh.

In the last decade, she's been a big favorite on the consciousness circuit and has appeared on *The Merv Griffin Show, Real People, America 2 Nite, Making It in L.A., First Annual Women's Comic Show* as well as her own TV show, *28 Minutes of Reality With Lotus,* where Bill Dana discovered her and asked her to pen "The Lotus Position."

Lotus now resides in Studio City, California, five blocks away from her producer-director husband, where she is raising a child who should be raising her.

HUMOR BOOKS

We Deliver!

And So Do These Bestsellers.